The Moustachapillar

JONTY LEES

eightbooks

The sun shone through the curtains,
Eric got up out of bed,
He made himself some breakfast,
It was marmalade and bread.

He went into the bathroom
And he stood against the sink,
When he looked into the mirror
His reflection made him think.

He wanted to be older,
He was bored of being young,
So he made some funny faces,
Pulled his cheeks, stuck out his tongue.

Then Eric found a picture
In a book he bought with cash,
Of an impressive looking chap
With a remarkable moustache.

Eric wasn't old enough
To grow one of his own,
So he tried out different things
That he had found around the home.

He tried a squirt of shaving foam,
And then a French baguette,
When Eric tried a ponytail
His sister got upset!

A cucumber was far too green,
A carrot was all wrong,
A drinking straw too skinny
And a hose pipe far too long,

Then later at the table,
Mum said, "What's that on your lips?
Eric stop that with your sausage,
Put it down and eat your chips."

So Eric went out playing,
Off to see what he could see,
A caterpillar crawled on him
And said, "Make room for me".

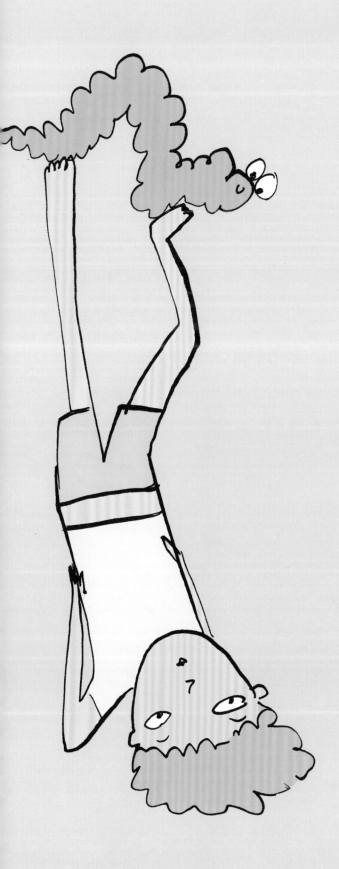

He crawled on top of Eric's head,
He crawled down to his toes,
The place he said he liked the best
Was under Eric's nose.

The two of them became good friends,
They did everything you do,
They went to see a movie,

And fed penguins at the zoo.

Then as they scooted through the park
They saw something ahead,
A sign was nailed to a tree
The writing on it read...

They sped off to the town hall
And they got there in a flash
And the chairman of the club said...
"A remarkable moustache!"

And "You've won the competition",
So they both felt quite a thrill,
Then they ate a lot of cake,
It was the cake that made them...

...ill

Eric's Mum came in to collect
Her son who wasn't well,
The caterpillar said "Goodbye"
And Eric waved farewell.

Time went by and Eric thought
About the friend he had,
He saw the moustache trophy,
And he felt a little sad.

He had to find his missing friend
Or he would be upset,
So Eric went out looking
At the place where they first met.

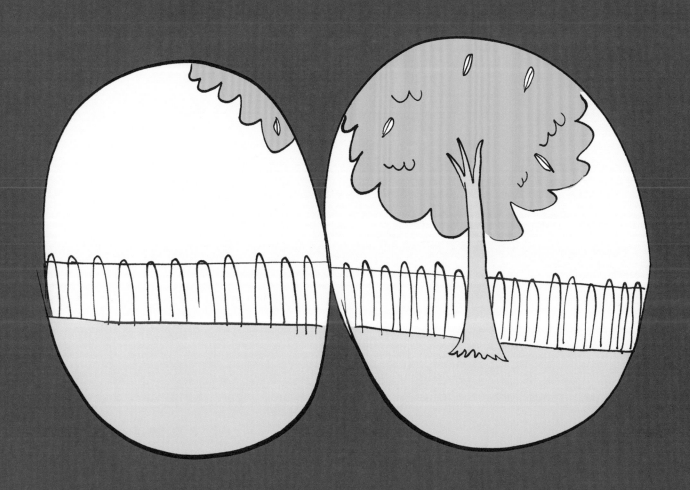

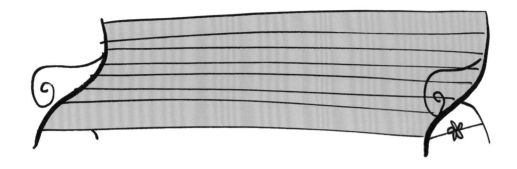

He found a little ladybird
Who didn't want to play,
He hopped after a grasshopper
Who said, "I cannot stay".

The bumblebee was busy
And the woodlouse made a ball,
He shouted, "Who will play with me?"
An old friend heard his call.

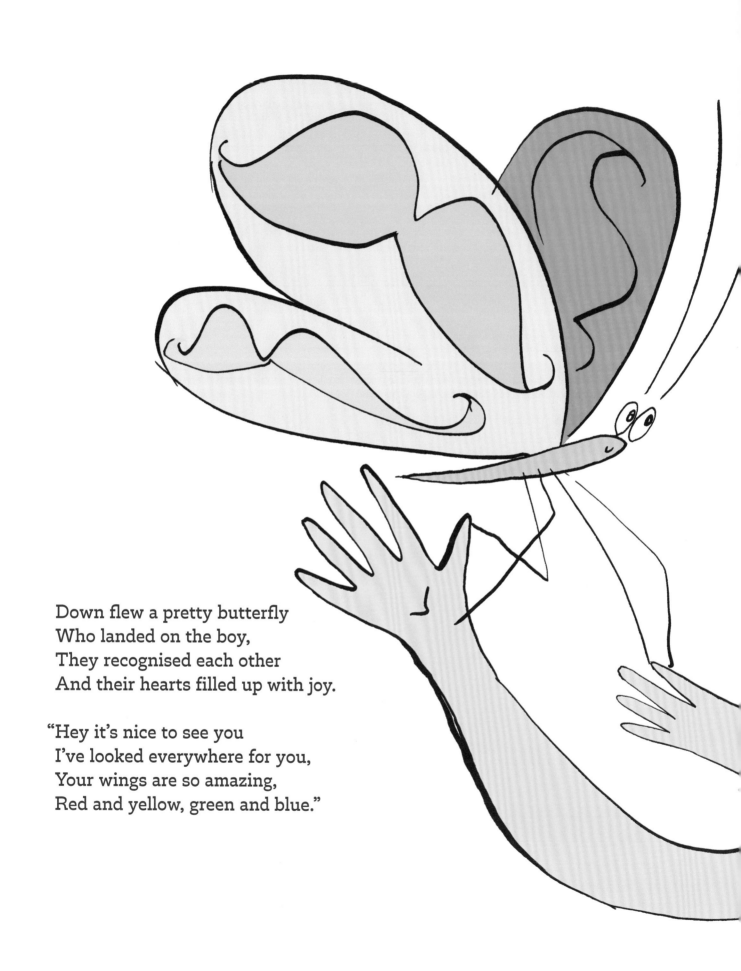

Down flew a pretty butterfly
Who landed on the boy,
They recognised each other
And their hearts filled up with joy.

"Hey it's nice to see you
I've looked everywhere for you,
Your wings are so amazing,
Red and yellow, green and blue."

"I like the look of flying",
Eric told the Butterfly,
So he made some wings from cardboard
And he jumped into the sky.

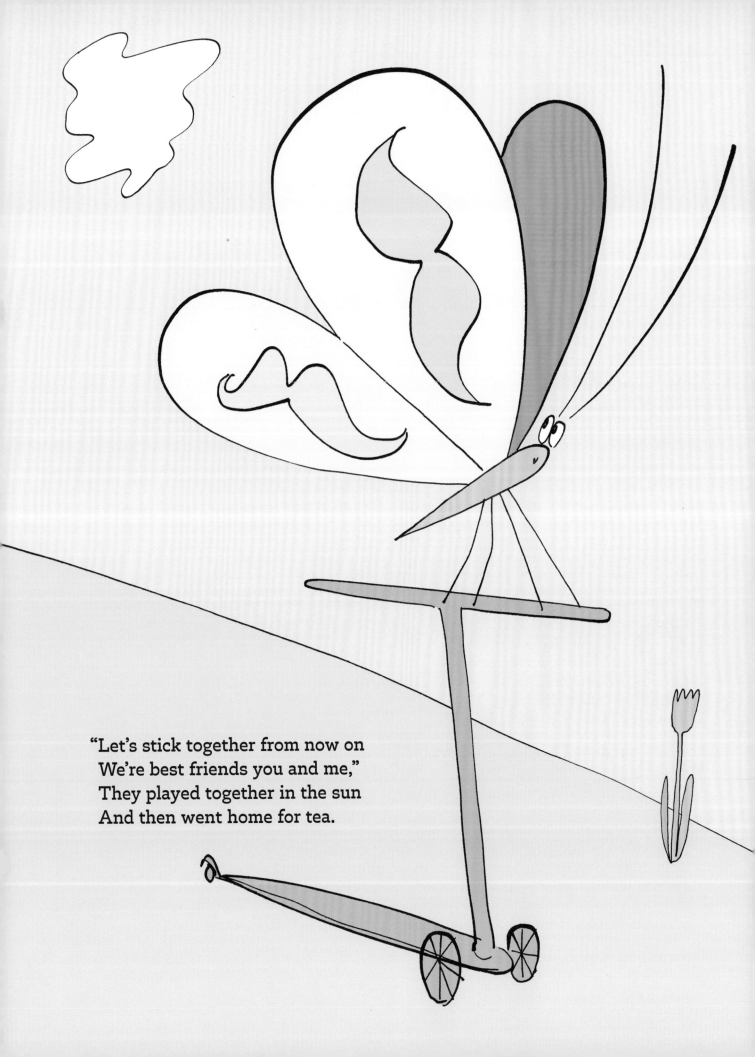

"Let's stick together from now on
We're best friends you and me,"
They played together in the sun
And then went home for tea.

For Mr Wilson

eightbooks

Published in 2011 by
Eight Books Limited
51 Ravenscroft Street
London E2 7QG
info@8books.co.uk
www.8books.co.uk

Paperback edition published in 2013

A catalogue record for this book is available from the British Library.

ISBN 978 0 9574717 0 2

Printed in China